Wolf Doctor

The Bite-Sized Shifters Series

By
Rose Bak

WOLF DOCTOR
© 2021 by Rose Bak

For all the vets and animal rescue folks

About This Book

When wolf shifter Colt Hanson plunges off a cliff, he's expecting to be roadkill. Fortunately, someone mistakes him for a dog and brings him to the town's veterinary clinic. He's not happy about waking up in a dog kennel, but when he opens his eyes and sees his fated mate, he knows things are finally looking up.

Dr. Valerie Lupa doesn't believe in fated mates, or any kind of mates for that matter. She's an independent wolf and she likes her life just the way it is. There's no way she's going to submit to Colt, no matter what her wolf side is telling her.

As the two shifters sniff around each other, the pull of their attraction proves too much to resist. With a little help from their friends, they just might be able to dip their paws into a relationship that will last longer than the full moon.

"Wolf Doctor" is book one in the "Bite-Sized Shifters", a series of paranormal romantic comedies you can read in just a few hours. Each book in the series is standalone featuring a mature couple, steamy scenes, a lot of fur and claws, and a guaranteed HEA.

Want a free book? Sign up for my newsletter[1] to be the first to know about new books and special sales. No spamming, I promise. Click here[2] to sign up for my newsletter and get your free book.

---

1. https://storyoriginapp.com/giveaways/62ee758e-068f-11eb-904e-c373f6014fe1

2. https://storyoriginapp.com/giveaways/62ee758e-068f-11eb-904e-c373f6014fe1

Colt

Twilight. Colt's favorite time of the day.

Stripping off his clothes, he took a deep breath, inhaling the scents on the air. He broke into a run and felt his body change mid-stride. In less than thirty seconds he had transformed from man to wolf.

Muscles and bone lengthening as gray hair sprouted all over his body, almost white in some places. His sharp canine teeth extended from his thickening jaw. He felt his tail grow behind him and he wagged it happily from side to side as he increased his pace, moving so fast his paws seemed to barely touch the ground.

Colt's senses were immediately heightened. His vision was sharper, his ears taking in even the softest sound, and his nose twitched with the wonderful scents of the pristine forest.

He headed through the woods, exhilarating in the feeling of free movement. His wolf loved to run. He hadn't shifted in almost a week. Too long. He needed this. He needed to shift and let his wolf run as much as he needed oxygen or food.

Speaking of food, he could use a snack. He scented a group of hares a mile away and headed in that direction at a gallop. His paws ate up the ground as he tracked the smaller beasts, stopping occasionally to sniff the ground and pick up their trail.

There, up ahead, he saw a flash of fur. He moved quickly, ears pinned back, as his wolf took over, the ultimate predator.

He could smell the fear on the hare as it took off, running for its life. Colt pulled his gums back in a canine smile. He loved the chase. The harder the capture, the better it tasted.

He sped up, following the hare instinctively as it took a sharp turn to the side. He pounced, leaping after the hare. Suddenly his feet hit air. And then he was falling. Fast.

Oh crap. He had overshot and gone right over the edge of the bluff. He could practically feel the stupid hare laughing at him as he tumbled down the embankment, scrambling but unable to stop his downward momentum.

He whined as his body hit the road below with a heavy thump.

Before he could recover he heard the squealing of brakes and suddenly he was airborne again. He landed on the asphalt a second time, feeling bones breaking and muscles tearing. He smelled the scent of his own blood and dimly heard voices as he struggled to stay conscious.

"Oh my god Dennis, you hit that poor dog!" The woman sounded upset.

"I'm not sure that it's a dog Sandy, it might be a wolf," someone, presumably Dennis, responded.

Not a dog, his wolf snipped in his head, clearly offended.

Really, that's your top worry right now? he asked his wolf.

Like all shifters, Colt shared space in his mind with his animal. He and his wolf shared not only the same body, but also the same consciousness.

He noted dimly that the humans who had hit him had exited their truck and were watching him cautiously from where they had stopped. He thought about getting up and whined again. The pain was terrible. It was impossible to move.

"He's bleeding and he's in pain," Sandy said, her voice sounding closer. "We have to get him to the animal hospital."

"There's no way he's going to survive," Dennis answered. "Let me get my shotgun out of the truck and I'll put the poor thing out of his misery."

Colt lifted his head in alarm, although it cost him dearly. He made eye contact with the woman, trying to communicate with her. He tried to make himself look sad and unthreatening. He did not want to die on the side of the road, and he definitely did not want to be put down by some random human with a shotgun. With his luck the guy would be a bad shot and make his injuries even worse.

"NO," Sandy said firmly. "You are not shooting him Dennis. Get the tarp. We'll put him in the back and drive him to the vet."

"He's a wounded animal Sandy," Dennis argued. "He may attack us, especially if he is a wolf."

Sandy continued to hold Colt's gaze. "No, he won't," she replied. "Come on, let's get him some help."

Colt passed out, not knowing who would win their argument. He just hoped it was Sandy.

He did not feel the couple cautiously wrapping him in a tarp and dragging him up into the back of their pick-up. He didn't feel himself sliding around in the truck bed as they raced to the animal hospital. He didn't hear the people loading him onto a gurney and wheeling his large body into the hospital. Both his body and his mind were completely shut down now, blissfully blocking the pain.

Then he felt it. A jolt of happiness and peace.

He opened his eyes, staring through the pain as an angel looked down at him. The overhead light glowed behind her like a halo. Thick brown hair framed her beautiful face. Her eyes were deep brown and impossibly kind.

"What happened?" his angel asked. Her voice made him feel calm. She seemed familiar.

"I think he took a header off a cliff. I think he came rolling down from up above. Suddenly there he was, falling onto the road right in front of us," Dennis explained. "Before I could stop, I hit him with my truck. I didn't do it on purpose, he seemed to come out of nowhere."

The angel's hand dropped gently to his head, rubbing him softly between his ears. He closed his eyes again, pressing against the warmth of her hand and whining softly. He had one thought before he passed out again. *Mate!*

Valerie

Dr. Valerie Lupa looked down at the large gray wolf resting on the gurney, closing her eyes briefly as she rubbed the wolf between his ears. He had lost a lot of blood and from the looks of it, had broken several bones. She was certain that he was also bleeding internally.

She sighed and twisted a long lock of her hair around her finger as she considered the situation. She would probably have to put him down. It was the humane thing to do. If he were a full wolf she wouldn't hesitate. But he was a shifter, that made the decision more complicated.

It wasn't like she could take him to a human doctor. There was no way to force his shift back to human form while he was unconscious. Of course, the humans knew of their existence, but mostly pretended that they didn't. It was easier to deny what their minds couldn't understand.

Human doctors didn't understand shifter physiology and right now they had no doctors nearby who specialized in shifter physiology. As a vet trained in working with shifters, Val often treated their kind. But this guy was in bad shape, she didn't want to cause him more pain unless there was a chance she could save him.

Suddenly she felt her wolf start pushing against her, trying to get out. Her wolf seemed frantic, and Val struggled to keep her under control. She couldn't risk shifting in front of the humans who had brought the wolf shifter to her clinic.

Mate! Her wolf roared in her head. *He's our mate! You have to save him! Save our mate!*

Well damn, that complicated things.

He's not our mate, she told her wolf sternly. *You know I don't believe in that mate bullshit.*

In her mind's eye she saw her wolf roll her eyes. Her wolf was a simple creature, but it never hesitated to share an opinion, especially when it Val wasn't doing what it wanted.

Then save him because he's part human, her wolf argued. *If you put him down none of his friends and family will know what happened to him.*

Her wolf was cunning, Val had to give her that.

All I can do is try, she responded, sending up a prayer to whatever god looked over the shifters. *Now go lay down so I can concentrate.*

Her wolf faded from her consciousness and Val got to work. After her assistant shuttled the humans out of the clinic Val gave the wolf shifter a shot of powerful sedative and got to work examining him, barking orders to her vet assistant Sandy.

Three hours later she stretched her back and sighed tiredly. She had done all she could do. She and Sandy had worked together to set his broken legs and she had operated to stop the internal bleeding in his abdomen.

Fortunately, Sandy was a shifter as well and understood what was at stake. Her other tech was human and might have questioned Val using such heroic measures to save a seemingly wild animal.

It was up to the magical power of the wolf now. Shifters had amazing healing powers, but the wolf's injuries were pretty serious. Besides his broken bones he surely had a concussion. At least he hadn't punctured a lung or gotten any major organ damage. She just hoped he would pull through.

They moved him into a large kennel, making him comfortable on an orthopedic dog bed and a nest of blankets. She hung the IV bag on the outside of the kennel door, checking to make sure that there was enough anesthetic to keep him unconscious throughout the night.

She needed to keep him sedated and in his wolf form to help him heal. As a human he would never make it.

Val sent Sandy home, checked on all the other animals one more time, and headed upstairs. She kept an apartment above the clinic where she could easily monitor their more serious cases. She even had cameras in various parts of the clinic so she could monitor her patients remotely from her place upstairs.

Val took a long hot shower, washing off traces of blood that had soaked through her scrubs when she was working on the wolf. It had been a long day, and she had just been getting ready to close when that human couple brought in the strange wolf.

Not just wolf, he is our mate! her wolf helpfully reminded her.

Val ignored her. She knew deep in her heart that her wolf was right, but that didn't mean she had to act on it. She really hoped that she could discharge the guy before he figured it out, or that he shared her views about the old ways. She didn't want to have to deal with some pushy wolf with romantic ideas about mates.

He already knows the truth, her wolf inserted.

It doesn't matter, she told her wolf. *I don't want a mate, and hopefully he doesn't either.*

Too bad, her wolf answered primly. *Because you got one.*

Colt

Colt groaned as he woke up, squinting against the harsh lights. His whole body hurt. Where was he?

He raised his head gingerly, looking around. He was naked and in his human form, laying on the ground in a nest of blankets, something soft beneath him. There were concrete walls on both sides of him. The air smelled of antiseptic and dog. He could hear a cat yowling in another room. What the hell?

He moved and felt a sting in his arm. There was an IV port taped to his wrist. His eyes followed the tubing to where it connected to an IV bag hung on the chain link door. Wait. Was he in a....dog kennel? Had someone taken him to a vet?

He looked around and saw a long row of kennels and several dogs looked back at him. In the center of the space as a large stainless steel table covered with what looked like medical instruments. Yep, he was definitely at an animal hospital.

Jolting in alarm, he rose to a sitting position, ignoring the head rush from his sudden movement. He looked around as he frantically tried to figure out how he had gotten there. The last thing he remembered he was chasing a hare. What had happened?

"Doctor Lupa! He's awake!" someone called.

He heard steps and saw a pair of long legs. A woman crouched down in front of his kennel, coming down to his eye level. He had an impression of the scent of citrus and something else, like the smell of rain in the forest. Colt looked up and met her concerned brown eyes. A shock went through him as if he had touched a downed power line. In that moment, he was struck with a profound sense of relief.

"Mate!" he growled, his voice rough like sandpaper. "You're finally here."

Hey eyes flashed in alarm so briefly he thought he imagined it.

"Hey Buddy, you're awake," she said softly. "How are you feeling?"

He ignored the fact that she was talking to him in that voice women used on babies and puppies. It was bad enough he was in a damn dog kennel like some common household pet.

"I feel like I was hit by a truck," he growled. "What happened?"

She smiled and for a moment he forgot how to breathe. She was beautiful, and her smile lit up her whole face. Her teeth were white with the tiniest bit of sharpness at her incisors.

"You got hit by a truck. After you fell off a cliff."

She stood up and he studied her. She was tall and strong, her wrinkled scrubs doing little to hide her muscular thighs and generous hips. Speaking of generous, she had an amazing rack.

Our mate has a strong body for birthing pups, his wolf pointed out happily.

Her thick brown hair was tucked into a haphazard bun and few strands fell against her stunningly beautiful face. A pen was stuck behind her ear as if she had put it there for a second and forgot about it. Her skin was flawless other than a small scar on the side of her chin. Her lips were full and generous, the lower one larger than the top one, with a touch of what looked like a clear lip gloss. She had the cutest pert nose between her large brown eyes, framed with long lashes.

Their eyes met and held, and he could see the animal lurking beneath the surface, calling out to its mate. He inhaled again, smelling her essence. Oh good, his mate was a wolf, just like him.

"You're my mate," he said, his voice full of wonder. "I've been looking for you all my life."

She rolled her eyes and backed away from his cage. "Don't be silly," she said, using the voice one might use with someone insane. "You're so gooped up on meds you probably don't even know your own name."

"It's Colt," he said drily. "Colton Hanson. Can you please let me out of this stupid kennel?"

She studied him. "Only if you promise me to move slowly and be careful. You're recovering from a serious injury. I would have drugged you more if I realized you were ready to shift back and wake up."

He nodded in agreement and she released the latch, opening the kennel door and holding out one strong hand. "Slowly now Colt. Let me help you up."

He didn't need the help, but he grasped her hand anyway, wanting to touch her. Her hand was small and lightly calloused, like she worked with her hands a lot. He heard her soft intake of breath as the electricity coursed between them. He knew in that moment his life would never be the same again.

Mate, his wolf said excitedly. *Mount her! Bite her! Claim our mate!*

How about we recover first? he suggested wryly.

"What happened exactly?" he asked his angel as he stood. His mate dropped his hand like it had burned her "I don't really remember much. And what's your name, mate?"

"I'm Doctor Lupa," she answered, and he wondered if she was omitting her first name as a way to distance herself from him. She didn't seem nearly as excited to find each other as he was. Her face was completely blank and expressionless other than the soft glow of her wolf in her eyes.

"Let's go into the lounge so you can sit down and rest while I examine you," she suggested. "You're still weak and recovering from a concussion."

He stepped out of the kennel and she looked down at his naked form, her eyes widening with admiration before she caught herself. Man and wolf preened in his head. He worked hard keeping fit, and now that he was about to turn forty, it felt more important than ever. He never wanted to be one of those potbellied wolves like some of his uncles.

"We'll get you some scrubs too," she said as she turned away from him. "You can't walk around naked."

He took a step and stumbled a bit as he got his footing. Now that she mentioned a concussion he realized he was the tiniest bit dizzy. His mate reached out to steady him.

Our mate has good reflexes, his wolf pointed out. *She is strong.*

With her hand on his arm and his IV bag in her other hand, the doctor slowly led him to the back of the building, calling for someone named Sandy to bring him some clothes.

A few seconds later a cute redhead strode over to them and handed him some clothes. "Here are some scrubs for our guest, Dr. Lupa."

He sniffed subtly and relaxed as she realized that the other woman was also some kind of shifter. She smelled like cat.

"Thanks Sandy," his mate said. "Can you administer the afternoon meds while I handle this?"

"Sure thing Doc."

His mate led him to what appeared to be an employee lounge then handed over the clothes that Sandy had given them. She helped him slide the IV bag through the sleeve as he pulled on the shirt, then stepped into pants. He tightened the drawstring to keep them in place.

His mate pointed to the couch. "Sit!" she ordered.

"You do know that I'm not actually a dog right?" he asked drily as he lowered himself to the worn couch. His throat was scratchy, and he coughed slightly with the words. She smirked.

"You must be thirsty," she said, moving to grab him a bottle of water from the fridge in the corner. "Here".

He took the bottle gratefully, twisting off the cap and drinking it down in one long gulp. Damn he was really thirsty. She returned to the fridge and got him a second bottle.

She took a few minutes to examine him, checking his heart, listening to his lungs, running her hands up the legs that had been broken just a few days ago. He was quiet while she worked, but he and his wolf both preened under her attention. His skin felt electrified everywhere she touched, and he could feel his heartbeat picking up the longer she was near him.

She carefully removed the IV tubing from his wrist, covering the rapidly closing wound with a small Band-Aid, and when she was finished she sat down in a hardbacked chair across from him. His wolf whined at her distance.

"So, Colt," she began. The sound of her voice immediately calmed down his wolf. "What do you remember about your accident?"

He frowned then looked around to make sure they had privacy.

"No humans here right now," his mate assured him. "Sandy's the only other one here."

He nodded, then relaxed back against the couch cushion as he tried to piece together what happened.

"I remember I was chasing a hare, and the little bastard went diving into the bushes. I didn't realize how close we were to the edge of the cliff and I overshot when I lunged for him. Next thing I knew I was tumbling down the hill."

He rubbed his head ruefully. "I swear I hit every rock on the way down." Colt frowned as the fuzziness cleared in his brain.

"I remember landing, then there was a screeching noise, then flying again, then people arguing about what do with me. Some dude wanted to shoot me, but there was a woman who protected me. Then it all went black until I heard your voice. How long have I been here?"

His mate leaned forward, watching him carefully. "Three days, since Friday. Today's Monday."

Colt sat straight up in alarm. "What? Oh my god. I lost three days?"

"We kept you heavily sedated after surgery, it was your best chance to heal," she explained. "I didn't want to take a chance if there was swelling around your brain."

"You did surgery?"

She nodded. "You had some internal bleeding but honestly it was not nearly as bad as I expected to find when I opened you up. There was no damage to your major organs."

"What else?" he asked.

"Both of your front legs were broken, probably from landing on the asphalt," she continued, "of course they're already mostly healed now."

Shifters had advanced healing compared to humans. "Other than that, and your concussion, it was mostly cuts and scrapes. Lots of road rash and scraped off fur. You were pretty lucky, all things considered."

He nodded. "I feel lucky to be here, mate," he told her with a serious look. He wondered if she knew he wasn't talking about the accident. Once again she had that brief flash of annoyance before she neutralized her expression.

"We had no idea who you were since you didn't have an ID on you. Are there people we should call?" she asked. "Someone at home who's worried about you? Maybe a girlfriend?"

Her voice seemed deliberately casual, and he wondered if he was trying to subtly figure out if she needed to get rid of a girlfriend before they were mated.

"No, I live alone. And I work at home too. My parents live in town but it's not unusual for me to go a few days without talking to them. Same for my friends."

She nodded.

"Mate....," he began.

She interrupted. "Don't call me that," she said, her voice sharp. "I don't believe in that mate shit."

"You never told me your name," he pointed out.

"Dr—-,"

"Your real name," he interrupted.

She sighed. "Valerie Lupa, although I go by Val," she said grudgingly, like she was giving him the secret nuclear codes instead of her first name.

"Valerie," he said, turning her name around in his mind. It suited her. "What a beautiful name."

A beautiful name for our beautiful mate, his wolf added happily.

She frowned at him, almost as if she had heard his wolf. The action made her brow crinkle adorably.

"You saved my life Valerie," he said gratefully. "Thank you."

"Well, I wasn't going to just put you down," she replied. "Not when I knew you were my....um, not when I realized that you were a shifter."

He cocked his head at her pause. She knew. She knew they were mates, just like he did. It wasn't just the concussion. She felt it, despite her protestations.

His father had told him once that finding your fated mate was like being hit by a thunderbolt, and it was always mutual.

He wondered at her resistance. Her wolf had to be an excited as his was. Most shifters were thrilled to find their destined mates. It didn't happen for everyone. Eventually a shifter might settle down with someone they were compatible with and live a happy life, but there was always a sense of loss to not have found their one true mate, the other half of their soul.

"Well, I'm feeling better by the minute," he told her. "I appreciate you taking care of me Valerie."

"Val," she responded.

"I like Valerie better," he told her.

She looked annoyed and he felt his cock twitch. Clearly that part of him was recovering just fine. Annoyed looked hot on her.

"Let me take you out to dinner to thank you," he said, giving her his most charming smile. That smile worked on every woman between the ages of eight and eighty. Except Valerie, apparently. She just deepened her frown.

"I was just doing my job," she rejoined quickly. "And while I appreciate the offer, I don't date my patients."

"Of course not, most of your patients are house pets," he rejoined.

Her eyes narrowed. "Since you're up and back to being in your human form I'm going to release you. I'm going to ask Sandy to drive you home," she said. "You seem to be recovering faster than I would have expected, but you need to rest for a few more days."

She held her hand up when he tried to interrupt.

"Take some ibuprofen every four hours to keep the pain down so you can heal," she continued. "Drink lots of water. Stay away from screens to help your concussion heal. And no shifting for at least a week. Your body has had quite a shock. You need to let yourself recover. If you start to feel worse, be sure to go see your human doctor."

"Mate...."

She stood up as if an electric jolt had gone through her seat and stepped away from him. He jumped up too, ignoring the pull on his arm as his IV bag fell to the floor.

He took a few steps to bring himself closer to her. She started to step back then stopped herself, straightening her spine and giving him a warning look. She wasn't short but he still had six inches on her, so she had to look up a bit to glare at him. His mate wasn't easily intimated.

He lifted one hand and ran his index finger slowly down her cheek. She shivered and closed her eyes for a long moment, then took a deep breath. When she opened her eyes again, they were once again shuttered and emotionless.

"You need to go home now Colt," she said, her voice a little shaky. "Sandy!" she hollered. "Can you come in here?"

The red-headed vet tech rushed through the door, looking between them curiously. "What do you need, doc?"

"Can you please drive Colt home while I finish my chart notes?" his mate asked. "I know you were about to head out anyway."

"Sure, no problem," Sandy said. "Let me just grab my purse Colt and I'll meet you out front."

"I'll go for now," Colt told her, his voice deep with promise. "But when I'm recovered I'll be back for you. We need to talk about what's happening with us."

Her eyes widened but she didn't respond other than shaking her head slightly. He leaned forward, placing a chaste kiss on her forehead. Val shivered.

"See you soon, little mate."

Valerie

"Your next appointment is here Dr. Lupa."

Val smiled at Debbie, the office manager for her practice, the glanced at the clock on the wall. "I thought my last appointment was at 3:00."

"Last minute addition," Debbie responded. "He's yummy. No, animal with him. Drug rep I assume. Sandy booked him while I was on lunch and didn't indicate the reason for his visit."

Val sighed. She hated the drug reps. They tended to drop by without notice, and they were always pushy. At least this one had the courtesy to make an appointment, not that it would help him. She didn't need some salesman with no veterinary training telling her what was best for her patients. Or best for his commission anyway.

"OK, send him back to my office then Debbie. But can you please do me a favor and come back in fifteen minutes with an emergency so I have an excuse to get rid of him."

"You got it Doc."

Val straightened her desk, arranging her files into one corner, and mentally steeled herself for a hard sell. Her wolf suddenly sat up, wagging her tail excitedly and pushing to get out.

Mate! Our mate's here.

She moved to standing and steeled herself for confrontation as Colt ambled into her office, closing the door behind him with a soft click.

Debbie was right, the man was yummy. Faded jeans hugged his strong thighs like a second skin, and a plain black t-shirt strained at his biceps. Thick brown hair, shot through with lighter golden streaks, highlighted his handsome face, and a bit of scruff darkened his strong jaw. His bright amber eyes were the only thing that hinted at the wolf beneath the surface.

He gave her a sexy smile and she saw a hint of a dimple on his left cheek. Damn it, she always was a sucker for a dimple.

"Hello mate," he drawled, meeting her eyes. She could sense his wolf looking out at her and knew her wolf was doing the same. She was tearing up Val's insides trying to get to her mate.

Be still damn it, she chastised her wolf.

She took a slow breath, trying to regulate the immediate physical reaction she felt seeing him. It had nearly been a week since she sent him home to recover from his accident, and she had spent way more time thinking of him than she wanted to.

Even when she managed to distract herself from thoughts of Colt, he appeared in her dreams. Long, hot, erotic dreams that had her waking up breathing heavily and feeling unsatisfied.

It didn't help that her wolf was obsessed with him, whining constantly to go find him and mate with him. No amount of running seemed to deter her. Slutty little thing.

"Colt, you're recovering I see," she said, congratulating herself on the way her voice came out calm and professional. She sat on the edge of her desk while Cole plopped his large body into the closest visitor chair, stretching his long legs out in front of him and appearing totally relaxed and at home.

The entire room filled with his unique scent and her wolf wiggled happily. She was immediately aware of him and willed her pulse to stay steady.

Mate him. Bite him. Her wolf pushed urgently against her.

"I am totally recovered," Colt answered. "Thanks to you."

"Are you sure you're feeling OK after everything that happened to you?" she asked, naturally going into doctor mode. "Any lingering dizziness? Other aches and pains?"

"Yep I'm much better. I just shifted for the first time since the accident and took my wolf for a short run," he answered. "My legs are still a little sore and there's some pulling from where the stitches were, but otherwise I think everything is good."

"Great, I'm glad to hear that" she replied. "I appreciate you stopping by to let me know, but I'm super busy and I really need to get back to work. Take care now."

She stood up and looked pointedly at the door.

"That's not why I stopped by Valerie," he said, staring up at her from his chair with hooded eyes.

"Oh. Um. Of course, you're wondering about the bill," she stammered before mentally shaking herself. "Don't worry about it, my office manager will send you something at the end of the month. Let my office manager know if you need a payment plan."

He shook his head, one corner of his mouth lifting in an amused smirk. He unfolded himself from the chair, watching her carefully. A predator watching his prey.

"You know that's not why I came. I'm here to claim my mate."

"What?" she squeaked even as her wolf wiggled with joy inside her. *Mate! Mate! Mate!*

She cleared her throat, grateful that her voice sounded stronger when she spoke again.

"Look Colt, I'm not your mate."

Liar, you know he is our mate, her wolf challenged her.

"You had a bad fall, and that's just the concussion talking. That mate stuff is just fairy tales mothers tell their pups as a bedtime story."

He took a step closer, and she resisted the urge to step back.

Bite him, her wolf urged, clawing at her insides trying to get out. Val kept her locked up with supreme effort, mentally smacking her wolf on the snout.

"It's not the concussion Valerie," he said firmly. "I know it, you know it, and both of our wolves know it. We're mates. I wasn't sure I believed in fate before, but now I know I was wrong. I feel it here."

He touched his chest over his heart, "I know you do too. We both know something is going on between us, something bigger than either of us. Something we can't ignore. I can see it in your eyes."

She lowered her traitorous eyes and gave into the instinct to move behind her desk, putting the furniture between them. He took a step closer, coming behind the desk to follow her, and she held up her hand to stop him. The air felt hot and heavy, the way it did before a storm, and Val struggled to keep herself from panicking.

"Stop that!" she ordered. "Even if I believed in that mate bullshit, which I don't, it wouldn't matter. I'm not on the market for a mate. I'm sure you're a great guy Colt, but I like my life the way it is, footloose and mate free."

He raised one skeptical eyebrow and reached down, shoving her chair out from between them without dropping his gaze. Her breath hitched as he grabbed her hand and pulled her closer to him with one tug.

They weren't touching, other than their hands, and yet her entire body was vibrating. It was like she was holding onto a live wire that was sending currents of electricity up her arm and straight down to her pussy.

It felt hard to breathe. Had someone cranked the heat? She felt a trail of sweat move down her spine. Maybe that explained why her panties suddenly felt damp.

She saw his nose twitch and knew he smelled her arousal.

Damn you body, why do you betray me?

Colt moved forward and grabbed her waist, spanning it with two large hands, ignoring her indignant squeak.

He lifted her up like she weighed nothing, and sat her on the edge of her desk, shoving her thighs apart with his hips. Before she could react, he moved to stand between her thighs, opening her wide and pressing his rock-hard erection against her core. Even though his jeans and her scrubs she could feel the heat of him.

He watched her for a long moment, his expression intense as he studied her face like he was memorizing every feature. He planted his hands on the desk at either side of her hips, then leaned forward, nuzzling her with his cheek against hers. Marking her with his scent as her wolf panted happily in her head.

She gasped as he dipped his tongue out and slid it down the heated skin of her neck. She shivered. It felt so good.

"Hey!" she said indignantly as she grasped onto her senses. She lifted her hands to his chest. "Back off!"

She intended to push him away, but somehow her hands just rested on his chest, his hard pecs flexing a bit beneath her palms. His heart was thudding wildly, the rhythm matching her own.

Meanwhile he took advantage of her open mouth and moved his head to capture her lips, sliding his tongue into her mouth as if he owned it. One large hand slid up to cup the back of her neck, holding her in place as he claimed her mouth.

Mate! her wolf chuffed happily. *Bite him!* Clearly her wolf had a one-track mind.

Colt's lips were strong but soft, and as his tongue slipped aggressively against hers, Val forgot her own name. Everything faded away except for the connection between their bodies.

She didn't know this man, yet it felt like she had known him forever. No kiss had ever felt this good this right. She returned his kiss with a fervor that would shock her when she thought about it later.

Her hands moved up his chest to grip his shoulders as Colt pulled her closer to him, his hands sliding down her back and kneading the muscles in her ass roughly.

Without any conscious thought she dug her fingers into his shoulders, breaking his skin even through his t-shirt. She realized that the tips of her claws were out as she scented the faint copper tinge of his blood. Her wolf was marking him, desperate to warn off any other females until they claimed each other officially.

He groaned approvingly and broke this kiss, moving his mouth to her neck, gently nipping his way down to her shoulder. She heard soft whimpers as he nibbled on her sensitive skin right where a mating bite would go. She was surprised to realize that the noise was coming from her.

"Valerie, you feel so good," he gasped, grinding his cock against her as she met him stroke for stroke. They were aggressively dry humping each other like horny teenagers, right there on her desk. She could smell her arousal permeating the room and knew he could too.

Before she could respond – if she could respond – he returned to her mouth, his kiss hard and claiming. One large hand gripped her hair, loosening her ponytail and pulling her head sideways to change the angle of their kiss.

Val lost herself in the heaven of his kiss. At this moment nothing else mattered but the feel of his mouth against hers. Their kiss went on and on as they explored each other's mouths and bodies. They were plastered so closely together she couldn't tell where she ended, and he began. And she didn't really care.

"Dr. Lupa, we have an emergency with one of the animals."

Debbie's voice came to her as if she were underwater. Before she could react, she heard her office manager barrel into the room. It was part of their usual routine to extricate her from pushy drug reps. Debbie had never found her dry humping someone in there before.

Val shoved Colt away from her with all her strength as Debbie gasped in shock. "Oh my god. Um. Wow. I'm so sorry to interrupt. I didn't know you were, um, busy."

"I'll be right there Debbie," Val called to her office manager she backed out of the room. Her voice shaky even to her own ears as she slowly moved to her feet. It felt like she was coming out of a trance.

What had just happened? Val was shocked. She had never in her life behaved like that. Never gave into her animal instincts, and certainly she had never made out with someone in her office before. Five more minutes and she would have let him fuck her right on her desk with her staff working in the next room. Damn Colt and his magic lips.

Suddenly she was furious at him for making her lose control. She reached up and smacked him on the side of the head. He yelped in surprise.

"Oh my god! That was not OK, you damn wolf," she snarled.

"You seemed to be enjoying yourself," he said mildly, adjusting himself. She looked down against her will and noticed his enormous erection trying to break through his pants. It looked uncomfortable. She licked her lips before she caught herself.

"You need to go now," she told him firmly. "I have work to do."

Colt watched her carefully before seeming to come to a decision. "I'll let you get back to work," he said. "But just so we're clear on my intentions little mate, I will be back. We will be together. It's fate. You can't fight fate."

"That's what you think," she snarled, her canines extending in anger, "I told you I don't want a mate, and I meant it. Now get the hell out of my clinic."

Val spun on her heel and headed towards her office door, heading to her fake emergency while her wolf whined pitifully in protest.

Colt

"Hi mate. How was your day?"

Val jumped at the sound of his voice. He purposely stood downwind, waiting to catch her by surprise as she closed up the vet hospital. He had spent the last twenty-hours reliving their hot make-out session on her desk while his wolf clamored to get out and go to their mate.

He knew she needed space. He wasn't sure what had happened in her past to put her off mating, but she was clearly skittish. Twenty-four hours was enough time for her to get used to the idea of them being mates, right? That kiss had to have convinced her. It had been hot as hell.

"Fuck off," she huffed, storming past him towards the alley behind the building.

Apparently twenty-four hours wasn't enough to accept their fated mate status after all. He followed her anyway. There was no way his wolf was going to let him give up so easily.

"How about dinner?" he asked as he caught up with her long stride.

"No."

"A drink?"

"No."

"Breakfast tomorrow?"

"No."

"Where are you going?" he asked curiously as she headed for a staircase in the alley.

She stopped so fast he nearly crashed into her. "Home. Not that it's any of your business."

"You live here?" he asked, looking dubiously at the rickety staircase. "That doesn't seem safe. What if someone jumped you? There's no one around at this time of night."

"And yet here you are," she said meanly, annoyance coming off her in waves. She pointed at her chest and added, "Wolf, remember? I can kick anyone's ass that tries to mess with me."

His cock hardened. His mate was a firecracker. He couldn't wait to fuck her. Couldn't wait to make her submit and accept his mark.

His wolf helpfully showed him an image of him taking Valerie from behind, screaming her release as he bit her neck. This was quickly followed by a vision of Valerie smiling at him softly, wearing his mate mark while her body was rounded with their pup.

Colt started to follow her up the stairs, but she turned suddenly and gave him a big shove. Caught off guard, he fell down several stairs and hit the pavement with a grunt. She was right, she was really strong.

"Hey!" he called from the ground. "Recovering from surgery, remember?"

She rolled her eyes and stormed up the stairs, taking them two at a time while they squeaked in protest.

"Go. Away," she shouted as she went into her apartment. "Leave me alone!" She slammed the door closed behind her so hard that the glass rattled.

"I know you want me, mate," he yelled after her from his spot on the ground.

Colt didn't need shifter hearing to catch her shout of frustration. He sat there watching her door for another hour, but she never came back out.

She must want us to woo her, his wolf suggested helpfully. *We need to show her that we will be a good mate. Show her that we will take good care of her and provide for her.*

He could do that. Colt headed home to create a plan.

The next day he showed up at the vet clinic mid-day with a huge bouquet of wildflowers. He strode up to the reception desk with a smile that women could never resist. Well, women who weren't Valerie anyway.

"Good afternoon Debbie," he greeted the woman who had interrupted their hot make-out session two days before. "Is Valerie available?"

Debbie eyed the huge bouquet flowers with a smile. "She's in surgery right now."

"Is she really? Or did she tell you to say that if I showed up?"

The woman's eyes widened in alarm. "Um. Well..."

He nodded. "OK I won't get you in trouble. But do you mind giving these flowers to her and telling her I miss her?"

She nodded, eager to help. "Of course, Colt."

He grabbed a piece of paper off the desk and scribbled his number on it. "Here's my number. Can you ask her to call me when she's out of her fake surgery?"

Debbie nodded, then gave him an appraising look.

"You're not some psycho are you?" she asked. "I like Dr. Lupa, you better not hurt her."

"Believe me, I would never hurt her," he promised. "I just want her to give me a chance."

They repeated the process for the next several days. Colt would show up with a gift for Valerie and an increasingly uncomfortable Debbie would lie and say that Valerie was in surgery. Colt would leave the gift with Debbie and extract a promise to ask Valerie to call him.

He could tell that the office manager was on his side, but his mate was stubborn and managed to avoid him.

He had also taken to stalking her ally in his wolf form at night, making sure no one bothered her as she exited the clinic and went up to her apartment. Colt knew Valerie knew he was there. Every night she would sniff the air, catch his scent, and send a frown his way, but otherwise she refused to acknowledge him.

On Friday he brought a large stuffed wolf with a bow for Valerie, and a box of chocolates for Debbie. The receptionist was clearly an ally, and as always, he left his phone number and asked Debbie to tell Valerie to call him.

"Tell her I'm going to keep coming every day until she calls me. Every single day, as long as it takes."

Debbie nodded. "I'll tell her," she promised.

Later that day Valerie finally broke down and texted him.

Valerie: Stop bothering me. Stop bothering my staff. Stop lurking outside my apartment.

Colt: Did you like the gifts, my mate?

Valerie: I threw them all out.

Colt: Liar. Debbie said you had them all stacked up in your office.

Valerie: I'm going to fire her.

Colt: I don't understand why you're being so difficult. We're perfect for each other, fated mates. It's every shifter's dream.

Valerie: Again – I don't want a mate. I don't need a mate. You need to leave me alone.

Colt: We don't have a choice. You can't fight fate.

Valerie: Yes we do. And I choose freedom.

Colt: If you would just take the time to get to know me you would really like me. I'm a very likable guy.

Valerie: Doubtful

Colt: Why are you so against mates? Most shifters go their whole lives without finding their true mate. We're so lucky.

Valerie: Why don't you go find one of those shifters and get lucky with them? I'm sure you can find some young wolf who believes all that fairy tale crap.

Colt: There is no one else for me know that I've met you.

Valerie: ...

Colt: How about this? Give me one date. Come for a run with me. My wolf wants to see your wolf. I'm sure your wolf is driving you crazy too.

Colt: Please, what do you have to lose?

Valerie: No

Colt: You know you want to.

Valerie: I really don't.

Colt: Yes you do, and so does your wolf. Say yes.

Valerie: ...

He thought she wouldn't respond, but five minutes later his phone pinged again.

Valerie: If I go for a run with you, will you leave me alone?

Colt: I can't promise that. My wolf is pretty strong willed. He knows what he wants and right now, all he wants is to spend time with his mate.

Valerie: ....

Colt: I can hear you thinking about it. Come on, it's just one run. Just to see how our wolves get along and confirm that we're really mates since you doubt it. We can kill a snack while we're out.

Valerie: Fine. One run. That's it. One hour. No humping. No marking. No mating.

Colt: Deal. We'll start with one date and go from there. I'll meet you behind your building in an hour, mate.

Valerie

She had to be crazy. Nothing good could come from them spending time together. Not that her wolf agreed. That little hussy was practically bursting out of her fur with excitement.

The longer she was apart from Colt, the harder it was to control the wolf inside her. Usually, she and her wolf coexisted peacefully, but that had definitely changed since they had met a certain alpha male.

Mate! Mate! We get to run with our mate!

Val waited for Colt outside, sitting on the steps to her apartment. Somehow it felt important to not let him inside her private domain.

She scented him before he came around the corner, her wolf immediately recognizing the scent that was distinctively Colt. Just like she scented him every night as he hung around in the woods that butted up against the ally, watching her as she came home.

He watches to protect us, he's a good mate. Her wolf was Team Colt all the way, that was for sure.

The man somehow managed to look devastatingly handsome in ordinary track pants and t-shirt with a picture of a superhero on it. His hair was tousled as if he had been running his fingers through it, and he had a couple days of scruff shadowing his face, making him look a tiny bit dangerous. Her mouth suddenly felt as dry as cotton.

"Hi Valerie." His voice was deep and warm, and she repressed a shiver. Yep, totally dangerous. He smiled at her with a look that had likely melted a million panties. Fortunately, she wasn't wearing any panties just now.

She stood up and nodded at him before moving to the edge of the woods that backed up against her property. It was a perfect place for her to run without any humans seeing her turn into a wolf or seeing her naked. Humans had such delicate sensibilities.

"Let's get this over with," she called to him over her shoulder. He chuckled at her sass but did not respond as he walked behind her.

She pulled her t-shirt over her head and dropped it on the ground behind a tree, then she kicked off her flip flops and yoga pants. Shifters as a rule were comfortable with nudity, and she was no exception. Still, she avoided looking at him and instead kept her gaze fixed on the woods as Colt removed his own clothes and piled them next to hers.

Without another word, she inhaled and called her wolf forward. Bones broke, lengthened, and reformed. Canines and claws extended as her muscles grew. Soft gray fur sprouted all over her body as she dropped to all fours. She relished the feeling of becoming stronger and freer, her animal taking over. She sniffed the air excitedly.

We are running with our mate!

It's just this one time, she reminded her wolf.

Her wolf scoffed at her but didn't respond.

She heard Colt changing forms behind her, but she still didn't look his way. Instead, she took off through the woods at a steady pace, knowing instinctive that Colt would follow her. She appreciated that he didn't try to take over and lead, the way most male shifters would do. He seemed content to let her set the pace and choose their course through the woods.

They couldn't talk in their wolf forms, but they communicated telepathically, sharing impressions more than actual words. Mated pairs were better able to communicate in their wolf forms, yet their wolves already seemed totally in sync with each other.

The ground was hard and warm beneath their paws, and they could hear the scurrying of little animals moving away from them as the crashed through the brush. It was...nice to run with him and she felt herself start to relax.

Val usually ran alone, and she found she was enjoying his company more than she would have expected. She was taken aback at the deep sense of safety and comfort she felt with him.

She led him deeper into woods and headed towards the river. It was a warm night, close enough to the summer solstice that it was still light out despite it being 7:00 at night.

Val loved running in the woods. The air smelled fresh and verdant, and other than the sounds of the creatures who lived in the woods they didn't run into anyone – human or shifter. There were enough shifters in and around town that it wasn't unusual for Val to run into someone she knew in these woods, but tonight it was peaceful. Just her and her m—.....just her and Colt.

As the trees thinned and the trail widened Colt sped up a bit, leaning forward and nipping at her flank. She turned with a playful growl and lowered to her chest with her butt up in the air, inviting him to play. Her wolf loved to play.

She got a good look at him in his wolf form for the first time. She had seen him in the clinic of course, but that had been clinical. Her focus had only been on his injuries. She hadn't had time to appreciate the majesty of his wolf. His wolf was gray like hers, but quite a bit bigger, with fur that was almost white around his snout and the tip of his tail.

Despite his size and his recent injury, he moved gracefully, landing softly on his big feet, and running effortlessly through the undergrowth.

They chased each other around, rolling and nipping and play growling like pups, until they grew tired. She led them to the river for a drink. Side by side they lowered their heads and drank their fill from the pure clean water that made its way down from the snow caps in the nearby mountains.

Colt threw himself onto the riverbank, effortlessly shifting back to his human form, and she followed suit. She sat next to him, leaning back on her hands and dipping her feet into the cool clear water. They were deeper in the woods than most humans ventured, so it felt safe to sit in the fading sunlight wearing just their skin.

After a while he nudged her with his shoulder, breaking the comfortable silence. "This is fun," he said, his tone almost cautious.

She turned and met his eyes. "It is," she acknowledged, even as she wished it wasn't true. It would be much easier if she hated being around him.

We love being with our mate, her wolf bragged in her head. *He's so strong and fun.*

The truth was, Val was having fun. More fun than she expected. Being with Colt felt so easy and natural. It scared her to death. Yet she felt helpless to turn away from his warm gaze, helpless to ignore the buzzing attraction that was slowly taking over her body.

Every cell in her body was focused on Colt. Her heart was thumping wildly, and she could feel her heartbeat deep in her core.

He leaned towards her slowly, a question clear in his eyes. Acting solely on instinct, she met him halfway, then closed the distance between them. In that moment, Val couldn't stop herself from kissing him. It was like his lips were powerful magnets, drawing her towards him.

Colt's lips were cold from the water but warmed up quickly as she explored his mouth. He let her lead and she deepened the kiss, exploring the recesses of his mouth. Only their mouths were touching, yet she could feel the heat of him on her skin as if he were caressing her.

They kissed for a long time, then they both groaned as they broke apart, each taking gulping deep breaths of oxygen. Acting purely on instinct, Val pushed him onto his back and leaned over him, one hand on either side of his neck. Right now she needed to kiss him again more than she needed her next breath.

As she drank from his lips, he lifted on hand and threaded his fingers in the tangle of her hair. Otherwise he didn't touch her, continuing to let her set the pace. He growled low in his throat as she explored the recesses of his mouth with her eager tongue.

For a long time, they were content to just kiss, letting their bodies communicate. Val sagged against his chest, laying partly over him, her sensitive nipples rubbing against the light fur on his chest. She felt is erection lengthening, poking against her hip.

Mate! Mate! Bite him! Her wolf was giddy at these developments, and Val struggled to hold her back from doing more than kissing Colt.

A bird squawked loudly, breaking the spell. She pulled back, looking down at him for a long moment as they both waited for their breathing to return to normal. He looked so handsome beneath her, his gaze hooded with passion.

"Cockblocked by a bird," he joked.

She grimaced as her common sense returned. How had this happened, she wondered. She had promised herself they would just run and then she could get rid of him, yet here she was, draped naked over his chest, kissing the stuffing out of him.

Val prided herself on always planning things out, never acting on instinct, instead letting logic and good sense guide her actions. She was always, always in total control. At least until now.

"Should we head back?" she asked softly, trying to mask the confusion she feared showed through in her own eyes. It was taking everything in her not to run away from him right now, but that would just excite the predator in him.

"Yep," he said, rolling over to his side and giving her a guarded look. No doubt he was picking up on the rapid change in her emotions. "It will be getting dark soon, and I already burned off that hare we ate."

He shifted on the ground with a loud cracking of bones and rolled over to stand on four paws. With a look over his shoulder he slowly led the way back to her place, apparently knowing the way purely on instinct.

She trailed behind him, freaked out about what had just happened and arguing with her wolf the entire way.

He's ours, her wolf insisted. *We must bite him. Claim our mate!*

Val's mother had thought she had found her mate. She claimed that they were true mates, and maybe they were, but Val doubted it. Her father had always been an asshole, pushing around her mother. Pushing around Val and his other kids. Blaming them for anything that went wrong in his life.

He was a jerk and a bully when he was sober, and when he was drunk he turned abusive. And he was drunk more often than not. Val and her siblings lived in constant fear of him and even though she would never admit it to them, so did her mother. They all walked on eggshells around him.

He was arrogant and demanding and only cared about himself. The bastard had never even officially married her mother although he had marked her early on, ensuring that no other shifter would touch her. Meanwhile her mother groveled for his attention, always trying to placate him.

Val hated him, and she hated her mother for putting up with him. "I can't leave him Valerie," her mother would say, "he's my mate. I belong with him." In her mom's world, love canceled out all bad behavior.

As soon as she turned eighteen Val had left home, and she hadn't looked back since. She had done well for herself, working her way through college and veterinary school before opening up her practice in a good-sized shifter town at the base of the mountains. Greysden had been without a vet for many years, and she had been eagerly welcomed into the town.

At thirty-six, she'd had a few relationships along the way, but none lasted more than six months. She mostly dated full humans, and always broke it off the minute they started getting serious. Val had vowed long ago that she would never tie herself to any man, human or shifter. She would never let herself get hurt.

She promised herself that she would never turn into her mother. She hadn't seen her mom in the eighteen years since she'd left home, and she rarely saw her siblings. Val talked to her mother on the phone about once a month, but the calls were usually brief. Her mother was always sad, always making excuses for her mate, and she had little to talk about besides her life with him. Mom didn't work outside the home, and her dad made sure she never made any friends, keeping her mother totally isolated and dependent on him for everything.

Val had learned early on that fate was capricious, and just because someone was your mate it didn't mean they would actually be nice to you. Sometimes fate just got it wrong.

Somehow she knew instinctively that Colt would never hurt her, and god knows she was stronger than her mom anyway. But she had no intention of getting stuck with some guy for the rest of her life. It was too much of a risk, and she didn't really know how to be in a long-term relationship anyway.

She liked her life just like it was. She liked coming and going when she wanted, without anyone wondering where she was or when she would be back. She liked having cereal for dinner and leaving the dirty bowl in the sink if she didn't feel like doing the dishes right away. She liked dancing in her underwear when a good song came on. She liked being independent.

Sometimes she got a bit lonely, but it was better than the alternative.

She found Colt incredibly attractive. She couldn't deny it. If he wasn't fixated on this mate crap she would definitely consider dating him, at least temporarily. She wondered if he would be up for that. Maybe if they spent some time together he would see that what he was calling the mate bond was just an infatuation. A sign of two people who had some incredible chemistry, nothing more. And chemistry would surely burn out after a while.

She and Colt could have some fun, as long as she was clear with him that it wasn't going to last. There was no way she could let it last. She could only offer him something casual.

He's our mate, her wolf reminded her. *There's no way this can be casual. That won't work for either of us.*

Damn it, her wolf was right. She needed to stick to her original plan: stay away from Colt.

That's not what I meant, her wolf chastised her.

New plan: stay away from Colt. Surely this pull towards him would ease if she avoided him long enough. Greysden was large enough that they had lived in the same town for several years without running into each other. She just needed to stay away from him until this mating fever passed and she could move on with her life.

She tried to ignore her wolf chuffing with amusement in her head. *Good luck with that.*

Colt

Colt could feel Valerie pulling away from him the closer they got to her apartment. Even without activating the mate bond yet, he was already able to sense her emotions.

He slowed his pace, trying to prolong their time together, as he tried to figure out his next move with her.

Bite her, his wolf suggested unhelpfully. *Show everyone she belongs to us.*

He knew he should give her some space. She clearly had some issues she needed to work through. He wondered what had made her so adamantly against the concept of fated mates. He had never heard of anyone rejecting the mate bond, at least not when both parties were shifters.

Colt had heard that it happened from time to time when one of the pair was a full human. Their ways were different. Humans had expectations about how long a relationship needed to be before getting serious. They tended to like longer courtships. They didn't have soulmates in the same way that shifters did, so they did not always trust the "love at first sight" concept that was totally normal to a shifter.

He was in over his head. He needed some advice. He should definitely give her space.

No space! Claim her! His damn wolf was getting annoying. He had no patience, no finesse.

They reached the edge of the woods where they had left their clothes. Valerie moved behind a tree to shift back and get dressed. He did the same, not speaking, waiting for her to make the next move.

They exited the woods and crossed the clinic parking lot, heading to the back of the building where the entrance to her apartment was. Dusk was falling and at this time in the evening, the area was completely deserted.

Valerie stopped and turned towards him, looking somewhere over his left shoulder. Her walls were firmly back in place.

"Thanks for running with me," she said, her voice showing no hint of her emotions. "I guess I'll see you around."

"Valerie..." he started.

"Look Colt," she interrupted. "I had a good time today, but this isn't going to work out. We both want different things right now. I know you want a mate, and I hope you find someone who wants that too. But as for us, we are not going to see each other again."

"Sure, we are," he said, infusing his voice with male arrogance to hide his irritation. So much for his plan to step back and give her space. His wolf was on board, of course.

Her eyes widened and she finally looked directly at him. A hint of red flush creeped up her face.

"You promised. One run and you would leave me alone."

"Actually, I explicitly told you I could not promise you that," he reminded her. "You just chose to hear what you wanted to hear."

She shook her head, and he patted the front pocket of his jeans where his phone was. "Should I pull up the texts to review my exact words?"

The flush on her face spread as she became more irritated. "Whatever. I know this is hard for someone like you to understand, but I'm really not that attracted to you," Val lied.

"Bullshit." Colt grinned at her. "You seemed pretty attracted to me when you were kissing me in the woods. A kiss you initiated, I may add. Admit it: you're just scared."

Valerie growled in annoyance and turned on her heel, heading towards the stairs. He easily caught up with her and grabbed her arm, turning her around. It felt like he spent a lot of time chasing this woman.

We always catch her, his wolf reminded him.

She opened her mouth to yell at him, but before she could speak he tugged her forward against the hard length of his body. Cupping the back of her neck with his other hand, he lowered his head and kissed her deeply, dominating her with his mouth.

He infused all of his emotions into the kiss: impatience, longing, irritation, desire, and most importantly, love. The truth was he had already fallen hopelessly in love with her, despite her desire to avoid him. She was the other half of his soul, in the way that only a shifter who had met their fated mate could understand.

Valerie stood stiffly in his arms for a long moment before giving up and relaxing into his embrace. He pulled her closer still, and she moaned as he rubbed the hard length of his erection against her.

She kissed him back eagerly, and her hands lifted to thread through his hair, tugging at the strands in a way that drove him crazy with desire for her.

When they kissed in the forest he let her take the lead. But now, he wanted to be in control. He wanted to dominate her until all her resistance to mating faded away. If he had to use her body to make that happen, that's what he would do.

He kissed her until the scent of her arousal permeated the air, until he was about a minute from taking her against the wall, then pulled back slowly with a Herculean effort. He needed to focus on the long game here. He needed to move past her resistance and convince his mate that they were meant to be together.

He pulled away reluctantly. Both of them were breathing heavily, their harsh breaths loud in the quiet of the fading twilight.

He stared at his mate. She looked a little dazed. Her eyes were unfocused, and her lips were swollen from the intensity of their kiss. Her hair was a tangled mess, and her shirt was halfway off her shoulder. She was stunning.

"You don't kiss me like someone who doesn't want to see me again," he said mockingly after he'd caught his breath. He couldn't help but poke her.

Her eyes blazed with annoyance. "God you're such an asshole," she raged as she stormed away from him and headed up her steps.

"But I'm your asshole. I'll call you," he promised.

"I won't answer," she rejoined as she opened her door and headed into her apartment. "I don't want to see you again."

"Tell that to your wolf, mate."

Her only response was the slamming of the door. His mate sure loved a good door slam.

Colt whistled to himself as he headed to his car. Their date wasn't a total failure. At least now he knew for sure that she felt the same as he did. No matter how much she protested, he could see the truth in her eyes. He just needed to figure out how to convince her to listen to what her instincts were telling her.

Her wolf definitely knows we're mates, his animal self told him. *Her wolf will help us.*

Colt: Good morning Valerie

Valerie: Why the fuck are you texting me at 7:30 am on a Saturday?

Cole: I missed you.

Valerie: What part of "leave me alone" wasn't clear to you?

Colt: How about breakfast?

Valerie: I can't, I'm busy.

Colt: No you're not, it's 7:30 in the morning

Valerie: ...

Colt: So, breakfast?

Valerie: ...

Colt: Lunch? Dinner?

Valerie: ...

Colt: Are you ignoring me?

Valerie: Would it help if I ignore you?

Colt: Nope. You're mine. You know it. I know it. Our wolves know it. No sense fighting it. Us getting together is inevitable.

Valerie: I don't want a mate. I don't want breakfast. And I don't want you blowing up my damn phone early in the morning.

Colt: OK I'll call you later

Valerie: Please don't. Do you always harass the women who tell you no?

Colt: If I actually believed you weren't interested I would, but I know that's not true.

Valerie: Actually, it is.

Colt: As I recall, you kissed me first yesterday.

Valerie: That was a temporary lapse in judgement.

Colt: So you didn't dream of me last night? Your wolf isn't scratching at your insides, begging to get closer to her mate?

Valerie: No

Colt: Liar

"So she's mate blocking you?" Stuart looked at Colt over his beer with an astonished look on his face. "I've always heard it's impossible to resist your true mate, at least if you're a shifter."

Colt eyed his best friend balefully. "Apparently, it is possible if you're stubborn enough. And my mate is definitely nothing if not stubborn."

Colt and Stuart had been best friends since grade school. When Valerie continued to ignore his invitations to talk or get together, he had invited Stuart to come out with him and help him drown his sorrows. They met up at their favorite bar and Colt caught him up on everything that had happened since that day he plunged off a cliff.

Stuart leaned forward, his muscled forearms resting on the tabletop. Despite his nerdy name, the wolf was all alpha male. Tall, handsome, and powerful. And so far, mateless.

"What are you going to do, dude?"

"I don't know," Colt said miserably.

"Tell me about her," Stuart suggested. "Let's see if we can figure out a plan."

Colt felt himself perking up. "She's beautiful. Fit and muscular, but also soft and curvy. Long brown hair, and the most beautiful brown eyes. And her smile, she doesn't share it often but when she does, it lights up a room. She's perfect," he ended with a sigh.

Stuart coughed to hide his laugh. "What's her name? I don't think you said."

"Valerie. She owns the veterinary clinic at the edge of town."

"Oh wait, is your mate Dr. Lupa?" Stuart asked.

"Yeah, that's her. Do you know her?" Colt asked curiously.

"Yeah," Stuart answered. "She's good friends with my sister. They go to book club together and I met her once at a party. I can see why you like her, she's awesome. Super smart. And totally hot."

Colt growled deep in his throat, leaning forward to glare at Stuart. "Stay away from my mate."

His friend raised his hands placatingly and tilted his neck to the side, baring his throat in submission. "Chill out Colt, I didn't mean any disrespect."

Colt relaxed back. "What am I going to do? It's painful to be apart from her, Stuart. Physically and emotionally painful."

"I have an idea," Stuart said, gesturing for the waitress. "Let's get another round."

Colt relaxed for the first time in days.

Valerie

"Val! So glad you could come!"

Val smiled and accepted a hug from her friend Susan.

"Thank for inviting me, it's been a while since you've had a game night."

Susan was Val's first friend when she moved to Greysden several years ago. The two had met at a book group held at the local library and immediately hit it off.

A fellow wolf shifter, they got together a few times a month, often going for a run together or meeting for happy hour. After so many years focusing on school, Val appreciated the opportunity to have some easy friendships with women her age.

Susan also loved to host periodic game nights where, as she put it, she brought together "interesting people and see how they react to competition". Susan was almost scarily competitive when it came to games, as were several of their friends.

"So, who's coming tonight?" Val asked as she placed her homemade guacamole on the table near the offerings from the other guests.

Game night was always a themed potluck; tonight, the theme was Mexican food. The table was overloaded with chips, taquitos, and a "make your own" taco bar. A pitcher of margaritas sat in the corner, ready for pouring.

"It's a small group tonight since this was kind of last minute ," Susan said, suddenly not meeting Val's eye. "My friends Jim and Nancy, my brother, and another friend of ours."

Val studied her friend. She looked kind of...shifty. Her energy was suddenly nervous.

"What's going on Susan?" she asked. "You seem weird tonight. Are you OK?"

Val felt goose bumps rise on her skin as her wolf started going crazy in her head. Oh crap, there was only one reason her wolf got that excited. One tall, dark, and alpha reason.

"Hi Valerie."

She spun around to meet the intense brown eyes of the man her wolf was insisting was her mate. He watched her carefully. She felt a wave of pleasure seeing him, and it really pissed her off.

"Colt! What the hell are you doing here?" she asked snappishly.

"He's the friend my brother Stuart brought," Susan said with forced casualness. Damn it, Susan knew. She knew that Colt thought they were mates.

We ARE mates, her wolf insisted sullenly. *You know it too.*

Val turned to glare at her friend. "Is this a set up?" she asked.

"Um."

"Damn it Susan, I wish you would have talked to me about this first."

"Would you have come if I had told you?" Her friend's eyes flashed in challenge.

"No. I have no desire to see this guy's stupid face again."

"Hey, I'm right here!" Colt protested.

Susan placed her arm on Val's hand, her eyes kind and soft. "I was so excited when Stuart told me that you'd found your mate…"

"He's not my mate."

"Yes I am."

"No you're not!"

Susan ignored their bickering. "When I heard that you were having…issues, I just thought it would be easier for you guys to get to know each other in a more casual environment," she explained. "I'm sure the human side of you needs to date instead of jumping right into a lifetime commitment."

Val wanted to be mad at her friend, but she knew her meddling was coming from a good place. If the situation were reversed, maybe she would do the same thing. After all, not everyone was anti-mate like she was.

"I should go."

"No, don't go. Please." Susan looped her arm through Val's and led her to the dining room table where tonight's game was set up. "Have a seat. I'll get you a margarita. Everything feels better with tequila."

Val greeted the others at the table and sat down, totally unsurprised when Colt dropped into the chair next to her. She studiously ignored him as Stuart reviewed the rules for tonight's game. She was surprised that Susan hadn't picked a partner game just to push along her matchmaking.

Colt slid his chair closer to hers and she subtly tried to move away but was stuck where she was by the table leg.

"Do you mind?" she hissed to Colt.

He just gave her a smile and moved his leg closer to hers. Bastard. Meanwhile her wolf was pacing excitedly inside her, thrilled to be touching her mate.

Having him this near was disrupting her equilibrium and she knew that Colt knew it. Her response to him was worse now that they had hung out together in their wolf forms. Worse after they made out several times. Colt was like a drug and she wanted him more after every hit. And she was worried that she wouldn't be able to resist him too much longer.

Val could feel the attraction simmering between them like a living, breathing thing. Her own breath seemed labored, like there wasn't enough oxygen in the room. She couldn't seem to slow her racing pulse no matter how many calming breaths she took. Her nipples were rock hard, pressing almost painfully against her bra.

To make things worse, he kept finding ways to touch her. Oh sure, it seemed innocent, a bumped hand here, a shoulder brush there, but she knew good and well he was doing it on purpose. Her wolf was pushing against her skin, dying to get out.

By the time they were finished with the first round of the game, Colt had practically moved into her lap he was so close.

While the others were engaged in conversation, she leaned over and whispered, "Can you give me some space please?"

Colt's eyes were amused. He knew the effect he was having on her, and found it amusing. He dropped on large hand on her thigh and squeezed it lightly, causing her breath to stutter. He leaned towards her and inhaled deeply. Val's face flushed as she realized that he could smell her arousal. Her panties were damp with it.

"Seems like you like it, mate," he whispered before gently nipping the shell of her ear with his teeth.

She elbowed him in the side, and he leaned back into his chair with a chuckle. Val looked up to see both Susan and her brother Stuart studying them with indulgent smiles.

"I don't know if you know this Val," Stuart began, "but Colt and I have been friends since grade school. He's a stand-up guy. He'll make a good mate."

"I'm so jealous that you found your mate," Susan added. "I'm starting to give up on finding mine."

"I don't want a mate," Val responded. "I appreciate what you guys are trying to do, I really do, but I'm really not interested in a relationship. I think I'm just going to head home."

"Val, no...," Susan started. Her friend looked distressed.

"You guys enjoy your game," she interrupted. "I'm super tired anyway. I had a really long day at the clinic. I'll just grab my Tupperware from you later. Good night all. Thanks for dinner."

Before anyone could say more, Val had grabbed her purse and shot out the door. She was halfway up the street when Colt caught up with her. Somehow she wasn't surprised. Part of her feared that he would follow her. And part of her hoped he would.

What was it about this guy? He had her totally mixed up.

She kept walking, moving quicky, ignoring him as he followed her like a shadow. He was so near she could swear that she felt the heat coming off his body. It had been hot that day and the night air felt hot and heavy. She was dripping with sweat, and her shirt was sticking to her back as she power walked back to her place.

She lived less than a mile away from Susan, and got home quickly, especially given how fast she was walking. She reached the corner of her building and turned around to tell him to leave, but before she got a word out Colt had grabbed her arm, pulling her to him.

This seemed to be a pattern with them. They had been here before, Colt chasing her and pulling her towards him, and Val losing hold of her resolve as soon as their bodies aligned. It was like a force greater than herself took control of her body every time they touched.

All he had to do was touch her and her brain shut down, ceding control to her traitorous body. She didn't understand why he seemed to have such power over her.

It's because he's our mate, her wolf said. It was true that she had never felt like this with anyone else. If any other guy manhandled her like this, she would have punched him in the throat. Yet with Colt, it just felt like...foreplay.

He paused for the briefest moment to meet her eyes, his own eyes glowing gold with his wolf, giving her a chance to push him away. When she didn't, his lips descended.

Val meant to push him away, honestly she did, but somehow her body and her wolf won the battle against common sense and she felt herself softening in his embrace instead. Colt threaded his hands in her long hair, holding her head in place, as he plundered her mouth.

She wrapped her hands around his waist, digging her nails into his back as the kiss went on and on. They had kissed before, but this kiss felt different. More powerful. More intense. Just more.

Maybe it was that her resistance was fading. Maybe Colt was right, and it was fate. Either way, between him and her wolf, they were wearing her down. She had a hard time remembering why being with him was such a bad idea.

"Valerie, I want you," Colt gasped against her lips as they broke for air. "I swear I tried to stay away and give you space, but I just can't do it. I want you too much."

She had never felt this intense of a reaction to any man before, and it scared her death. He wasn't the only one who was struggling to stay away.

She could feel the hard length of his erection pressing against her lower belly, and she knew her panties were completely soaked.

But then he started kissing her again, and she pushed her doubts away. All she could do it hold on. She just could not force herself to fight him anymore. Nor could she fight herself.

Colt walked her backwards towards the steps to her apartment, stopping at the bottom. His eyes were soft and loving, his expression tender. That affected her more than anything else.

"Invite me up Valerie. Please." His voice was deep and rough like someone had taken sandpaper to his vocal cords. "Be with me tonight."

Invite him up, invite him up, her wolf chanted eagerly.

She hesitated for a moment, but the truth was, she wanted him. She wanted him more than she had ever wanted anything ever before. And tonight, with the air thick and warm around them and her arms tight around his lean waist, she wanted to throw caution to the wind. She wanted to give in to her wolf, and just this once, do something solely because it felt good, no matter what the consequences.

"I want you to come up," she whispered. "But only for tonight. That's all I can give you Colt, one night. Nothing more."

"Sure," he said skeptically. "One night. I'm sure that will be enough. No problem."

Before she could respond to his sarcastic rejoinder he leaned down and threw her over his shoulder, giving her ass a sharp tap as he carried her up the stairs.

"We'll see how that plan works out for you and your wolf, mate."

Colt

Colt put Valerie down so she could unlock the door, but as soon as the door swung open, he was moving. Closing the door closed behind them, he pushed Valerie against the wall and crowded close to her, one hand on each side of her head.

Her eyes were wide and excited. She pressed her breasts against his chest with a low moan. For once he didn't feel those walls she kept up around her as protection. She was as open and eager as he had ever seen her. Her desire for him was clear.

Mate, his wolf reminded him, as if he could forget. *Mount her.* His wolf didn't seem to understand the need for foreplay.

Colt leaned in and covered Valerie's mouth with his own. Their tongues met, dueling as they each sought control. Already his cock was so hard that his zipper was pushing painfully back on his erection. He ground it against her, earning him a long moan as she tilted her pelvis to meet him.

He reached down and grabbed her thighs in his large hands, lifting them up and wrapping them up around his waist. He held her between him and the wall. The change in position brought the heat of her core right where he wanted it. He didn't have to be a shifter to smell their mutual arousal in the air.

Valerie slid her fingers through his hair, tugging firmly on the strands in the way she had that drove him crazy. The bite of pain only heightened his arousal. His heart was pounded so hard he almost felt dizzy. She ground against him, locking her ankles behind him to keep him close.

"Bedroom," he gasped.

"Down the hall."

He carried her towards the bedroom, kissing her as he walked. Colt put her down again as they entered the bedroom. He had a quick impression of a warm and inviting space, but his attention immediately went to the king-sized bed in the middle of the large room.

"Strip," Valerie ordered. He loved it when she was bossy.

His heart stuttered as he looked back to see her already removing her own clothes. He had seen her naked before of course, when they shifted, but somehow this seemed different. More intimate. He couldn't help but admire her pert nipples, her trim waist, the swell of her generous hips.

Colt reached behind himself to pull his shirt off, then slid his jeans and boxers down in one big push and kicked them aside. His cock jutted out proudly and he heard Valerie growl low in her throat, her eyes fixed on his girth.

Our mate likes what she sees, his wolf preened proudly.

He placed one hand on her chest and gently pushed her towards the bed, settling her on her back before pulling her hips back towards the edge.

He kneeled down between her thighs and tasted heaven. One long lick of his mate's sweet cream and he knew he was ruined for any other woman.

He licked up and down her slit in long slow laps, his tongue flat against her, and held her thighs open with his hands, gripping her hard enough that he would probably leave a bruise. He loved the idea of marking her, however he could.

Bite her, bruises fade but the mate mark lasts forever, suggested his wolf.

Valerie thrashed on the bed, alternately moving closer to him, and trying to move away as he increased his efforts. He held her firmly and thrust his tongue into her channel, fucking her with his tongue the way he longed to do with other body parts.

Colt moved one hand to press down on the top of her neatly trimmed mound, stabilizing her thrusting pelvis. He used his thumb to press and circle her clit. Valerie was making some kind of a sound that was a cross between a whine and a moan. It was hot as hell.

He pressed his cock against the edge of the mattress trying to relieve the pressure and keep himself from shooting his load in his pants like some teenage wolf. He had been with several women over the years, but nothing had ever felt like this. It was electric. Life changing.

He increased the pressure on her clit as he continued thrusting inside her with his tongue, working her body as if they had been together a million times. Somehow he knew instinctively what to do to bring her the maximum amount of pleasure. He felt her tighten around his tongue a second before her entire body bowed off the bed.

"Colt!" His name ended in a long wail.

In his peripheral vision he saw her claws extend, ripping the sheets as her orgasm moved through her. He kept licking and stroking her until her orgasm was finished, and she sagged into the mattress, trembling with aftershocks.

Colt looked up to meet her eyes, licking her essence off his lips. Valerie's eyes glowed with her wolf, closer to the surface than he had ever seen it while she was in human form.

"Come here!" she ordered, motioning him with a crook of her finger. His heart soared as he realized that she wasn't done with him yet. Thank god.

She scooted back towards the headboard and he crawled up her body, sliding between her legs. She let her knees fall open to the side.

He settled in between her legs, grinding his pelvis into the mattress, and stretched his neck so he could bring one engorged nipple between his lips. They were hard and flushed red against the creaminess of her breasts. He latched on to one, biting down and sucking at the same time. Valerie made a whining noise that told him she liked what he was doing.

He continued sucking and biting her until she was writhing beneath him, then moved to the other breast, giving it the same attention, sucking and biting the nub into a hardened peak.

When he couldn't take it anymore, he licked and kissed his way up the rest of her body, moving to cover her with his bulk and keeping her pressed against the mattress. He dominated her, and he could tell from the heat of her gaze she didn't mind that at all.

He nipped the skin of one breast, then bit and licked his way up to her lips. She met his kiss eagerly and lifted her legs to wrap around his waist once again, pulling him closer to her moist heat.

He lined up his cock with her opening and without a word, thrust all the way inside her with one hard thrust. She gasped against his lips, then lowered her hands to his ass. He could feel the tips of her claws extend and dig into the skin there as she pulled him closer.

He began to thrust in and out of her tight heat while mimicking the movement with his tongue. Valerie matched his rhythm, her hips rising to meet his on every thrust, their pelvises slamming together with every joining.

Colt lifted behind her knees and widened her legs, pulling them away from his back. He moved her legs until her calves were resting on his shoulders, then slid his hands beneath her shoulder blades. This change in position allowed him to get deeper inside her, his pelvis grinding against her clit with every hard thrust as he completely surrounded her.

"I'm close," Valerie gasped. She tightened her internal muscles around him, making him groan deep in his throat.

His fangs pressed against his gums. He leaned down and nipped her lips with the very tips of his fangs, and he felt her explode beneath him with a long moan that had his balls tightening.

His spine tingled in warning and then he was right behind her, his orgasm ripping through his body with the force of a freight train. He pounded into her once, twice, three time more before he pumped his seed deep inside her womb.

Colt felt a moment of pure ecstasy as they continued moving together. He never knew it could be like this. So intense, yet so perfect.

"Mate!" he growled.

His fangs extended again and his wolf took over as he lost control. He dropped his head to bite the flesh at the point where her shoulder met her neck. He broke the skin, fangs tearing through down to the muscle, permanently marking her as shifters had marked their mates for millennia. He could taste the copper of her warm blood in his mouth.

Valerie screamed and their orgasms went super nova, extending their pleasure for long moments. The magic of the mate bond flew through them, connecting them on another level, activated by his bite.

As they finally came down, Colt collapsed on top of her, his entire body filled with complete happiness.

She's officially our mate now! His wolf was ecstatic, and so was Colt. Everything was going to be OK now. He was sure of it.

Valerie

She was a puddle. She lay there totally boneless, her mind completely empty. For the first time in her thirty-six years, she was totally and completely at peace.

Valerie lay flat on the bed, waiting for her heart rate and breathing to return to normal. She was hot and sweaty, and Colt was laying on top of her like the world's heaviest blanket, licking her neck to seal her wound.

Wait! Licking her neck? Wound?

She searched her mind and felt it: the mate bond. A connection between them like an invisible cord. Val had heard about the mate bond, read the stories, but she always assumed it was a myth. But no, it wasn't a myth. She could feel it pulsing between them, connecting them forever.

We're mates now, her wolf confirmed happily. What the hell?

Val pushed Colt off of her with a hard shove and sat up while he looked at her in confusion. She reached up to feel her neck and felt a swollen wound, already closing with her super shifter healing. It felt hot and electric to her touch, proof of the magical bond between them now.

"What did you do?" she shrieked.

Colt rolled over to his back, crossing his hands behind his head, looking like he didn't have a care in the world. "What do you mean?"

"You bit me?" she yelled. "You freaking bit me! Why on Earth did you bite me?"

We are mated now, her wolf cheered. *Bite him back now. Make the bond stronger.*

Ignoring the happy rumbling of her other side, she jumped out of bed and looked in the mirror. Maybe she was mistaken. Maybe it was really just a giant hickey. She stared at the red spot on her shoulder hopefully.

Nope, there was definitely a mate bite on her neck. They looked and felt very distinctive. The mate bite connected their souls through the supernatural magic that gave them their powers. Damn him!

In the shifter world, a mate bite signaled commitment. It was the same as getting married in the human world, although shifters generally did that as well. No sense passing up the opportunity to have a big party and get some gifts.

The mate bite acted as a signal to every other shifter that someone was in a committed relationship. It blended the scents of the biter and the bitee, so no other shifter would get near someone who was mated.

It was permanent. Way more permanent than a wedding ring. It was exactly what she always promised herself to avoid. She had let her guard down once, one time in her entire adult life, and look what happened. She was mated to some guy she had known for a couple of weeks. Some guy who believed in the traditional shifter happily ever after.

Val had never been so angry in her life. She was vibrating with rage, her blood pressure skyrocketing, her vision tinged with a red haze.

"Get out! Get out now!"

She grabbed a throw pillow off a chair and whipped it at Colt's big stupid head.

He howled at her. "Mate! What the hell is the matter?"

She shoved on a pair of sweats and a t-shirt before stalking over towards the bed. She grabbed his ankle, trying to pull him off her bed. He weighed a ton, and she was only able to pull him towards the edge, but at least her effort made him stand up.

She tried to ignore the naked magnificence of her, um, Colt. God he was a fine specimen. Lean and muscular. This was supposed to be a one night thing, not something that would tie her to some random guy for the rest of her life.

He's not some random guy. He's our mate! Her wolf's reminder just made her angrier.

"I can't believe you bit me without my consent," she yelled, cringing internally as her voice got higher with every word. Another octave or two higher and the dogs in the clinic downstairs would hear her.

"I got carried away," he defended as he jerked his pants back on, looking wounded at her response. "It was going to happen anyway. What's the big deal?"

"What's the big deal?" she shrieked. "What's the big deal?!?!?"

She picked up a plastic bottle of lotion from her dresser and whipped it at him, feeling a sense of satisfaction when it hit him hard on the chest. He grunted in reaction.

"I never agreed to being mated! You know it's against our shifter rules to do that!"

"You knew when you agreed to have sex with me that we were taking the next step," he told her, his voice hardening. "You knew going in what we are and how I felt."

Val picked up her hairbrush and winged it at his head, but he moved too quickly, and it flew harmlessly past his ear. Fucker.

"I said, very clearly I may add, that this was a one time thing," she reminded him. "I told you, I only wanted tonight."

"Well, you can lie to yourself all you want mate," he growled, "but we both knew going in that us making love would change everything. We're fated mates. It could never be casual. You know this as well as I do."

"It was fucking. Nothing more," she argued. "That's all I agreed to. That's all I wanted."

"I can see you need some time to process everything," Colt responded, using that placating voice people use when confronted with someone who is completely hysterical.

She grabbed the first thing she could reach—a votive candle—and hurled it at him. It connected with his head with a satisfying thump. He grunted in annoyance.

"God damn it mate, stop throwing shit at me."

Stop hurting our mate, her wolf agreed. She of course was totally cool with Colt marking them.

In some part of her brain Val couldn't believe she was acting like this. She had never been this angry in her life. Certainly, she had never thrown things at someone before. It was either that or throttle this guy.

Val stalked towards him, her claws extended and eyes burning fire. Her chest was heaving with anger and exertion.

"I. Am. Not. Your. Mate."

She pushed his shoulders, hard. "Get the fuck out of my house. And stay away from me. I never want to see you again."

He had the audacity to look hurt. "You don't mean that. We're mated now. We belong together. I'm yours, and you are mine."

She shoved him again and he took another step back.

"Get. Out."

He backed up toward the door like he was afraid to turn his back on her. Smart man.

"OK, I'm going to give you some time Valerie, but you and I both know that you can't ignore the mate bond."

She ground her teeth as he continued, "It was hard enough before, but now that I've bitten you and the bond has activated, our wolves won't let us stay apart, no matter what we think. Resisting this is useless."

"Aaarrghhh!" she yelled, looking for something else to throw at him.

"I'll just give you some time to cool down," he told her, his voice still infuriatingly calm, which just pissed her off more. He turned on his heel and stalked out of her apartment without another word.

Val clenched her fists and screamed a long, primal howl. She was going to kill him.

Colt

He had fucked up. There was no way around it. If he had been thinking clearly he would never have given Valerie the mate bite. At least not yet. He knew she needed more time.

His mate was not one to be rushed into anything, especially something as permanent as mating. Her wounds were too deep, and her walls were too high.

Unfortunately, his wolf didn't care about taking time. His wolf only wanted to be connected to his mate. He had wanted to tie her to them before she got away. Before another wolf touched her.

Wolves were simple creatures. Eat. Sleep. Run. Mate. Everything else was background noise as far as they were concerned. Humans made things way too complicated.

If Colt had been in his right mind he might have been able to hold himself back from marking her, but in the midst of the most mind-blowing sex of his life, caution and logical thought had gone right out the window.

He felt dejected as he stalked back to his car, which was still parked outside of Susan's house. He had fucked this up, but he and Valerie were meant to be together. He just needed to convince her of that.

Surely fate had a plan for them, right? A plan yeah, that's what he needed. Should he continue to push, or give her some space and wait for her to catch up with the wolf inside her?

Mate's wolf wants us, his wolf confirmed.

It had about two hours since they had left the game night at Susan's house, but it was still relatively early. He glanced at his watch. It was just before 10 o'clock and he could see Stuart's car still in the driveway. He decided to knock.

He was glad to see the other guests had gone, and it was just Stuart and his sister Susan. He didn't need anyone else to witness his humiliation.

"Oh, hey Colt," Susan gestured him inside. "We were just cleaning up. You and Val missed a very competitive final round. I thought people were going to bring their claws out."

Colt threw himself onto a kitchen chair with a long sigh. Susan and Stuart exchanged a look.

"You want a beer, man?" Stuart asked.

"Yeah," he mumbled as he dropped his head on the table. He heard his friend slide a beer in front of him, but he didn't look up. It hurt too much.

"I smell some mating, so I take it that you and Val had some fun after you left," Susan said, the smile evident in her voice. "What happened? You couldn't satisfy your mate? Maybe she was hoping for something a little bigger?"

"I satisfied her just fine," he growled. He sat up and glared at his friend's sister.

"What happened?" Stuart asked gently.

"I got a little, um, overexcited," Colt explained. "I bit her. Marked her and activated the mate bond. If I had been thinking clearly I would have known it was too soon for her, but my wolf was all ready to go..."

"Well, it was bound to happen," Susan responded. "You two were giving off crazy hot pheromones. I was getting hot and bothered just watching you together. So much smoldering. I'm going to need some time with my vibrator tonight to settle down."

"Susan, please," Stuart moaned. "A brother does not want to hear that."

He focused his attention back on Colt. "So how did it go down?"

"I walked her home and she just ignored me the whole time. We got to her property and I kissed her, and then she was like, OK, let's go."

"That sounds good," Susan interjected.

"But then she was like, oh it's just this one night, I don't want anything more, and I said yeah good luck with that."

The siblings snickered.

"Then I went upstairs to her place, and everything was great, we were totally in sync. It was perfect. Totally life changing," he continued, even as he realized he was talking like a teen in some angsty film.

"Until the haze lifted, and she realized that I had bitten her in the heat of passion. Next thing I know she's chucking things at my head. And she has really good aim too."

"She played varsity softball in college," Susan added helpfully.

"I have to fix this," he sighed, dropping his head back to the table with a loud thunk. "I just have no idea how."

"Look man, she's your mate. It's meant to be," Stuart reminded him. "You'll find your way back to each other. There's no way your wolves will let you stay apart."

"I hope you're right Stuart, I hope you're right."

Colt waited until the next afternoon to contact her. He kept looking at his phone, hoping for a message from her with all the eager longing of a teenager waiting for a text from their crush. When he couldn't take it anymore he decided to text her rather than showing up at her place uninvited. At least she couldn't throw things at his head that way.

Colt: I'm sorry.

Colt: Just to be clear, I'm not sorry I mated you, I'm just sorry I didn't wait for you to catch up

Colt: Can we talk?

Colt: Please, I need to talk to you. At least let me know you're OK.

Colt: I miss you.

When she didn't respond he tried to call her, but of course she didn't pick up. Not that he was surprised. The next time he called, the phone rang once and went to voicemail, telling him that she had shut off her phone.

He tried to distract himself, working in his home office and trying to finish up some projects for one of his clients. His wolf whined incessantly, a constant hum in his head.

Mate. Mate. Mate. Need our mate.

The only consolation was that he knew that Valerie was going through the same thing. All shifters had heard the tales of what happened when people were kept away from their mates, especially in the early days of their joining. The animals inside would drive them crazy until they got what they wanted – being reunited with their mate.

If they didn't get together after finding each other, eventually a shifter would go feral. It was too hard to be apart, especially for pack animals like wolves.

He debated going after her again, but so far he had done all the pushing. He was the one always putting himself out there. She knew where he stood. Knew how he felt, and what he wanted. Now he needed her to give a little too. If he could just give her some time, surely she would come around.

Run. Let's go for run then.

After a long day of ignoring his wolf's demands to go find his mate, Colt decided to go for a run. It was the best way to wear out his wolf, and his own body, so that they could both get some sleep tonight.

Everything would look better after a good night's sleep. Then he could figure out his next move to winning over his mate.

He headed out in his skin, running through the streets in the direction of the forest that ran along two sides of the town. It was one of the reasons his wolf ancestors had settled here. The combination of old growth forest and a relatively isolated location meant that shifters could live peacefully, away from the prying eyes of the humans who didn't understand their ways.

Shifters always did better when they were close to nature. City dwelling shifters tended to be way less happy.

Once he was a little way into the forest Colt stopped to remove his running clothes, tucking them and his shoes under a bush where he could pick them up later. He didn't worry about someone stealing his stuff. The humans rarely ventured to this part of the forest and every shifter knew that your stash of clothes was not to be messed with.

Colt took a deep breath and called his wolf forth, moving through the magical transition of his body from man to wolf. In this form, he usually took a backseat to his wolf, letting it off the leash to run and play in the woods. Of course, letting his wolf be in charge is exactly how he took a header off a cliff and got hit by a car.

That's how we met our mate, his wolf reminded him. *Totally worth it.*

He ran hard, his paws scrabbling on the hard dry ground, panting as he ran like the hounds of hell were behind him. He wanted to be so exhausted that neither he nor his wolf were thinking about their mate when they were done.

Mate! Mate!

Yeah, like that, he thought drily.

No, our mate. She is here!

Colt sniffed the air and sure enough, he sensed the unmistakable scent of his mate. She was close by. He rounded a bend and there she was in her wolf glory, running so hard they appeared to be unaware of their surroundings. Clearly they both had the same idea.

Valerie skidded to a stop, panting hard as she stared at him with narrowed eyes. Her tail was sticking straight out, as if she were spoiling for a confrontation.

Colt dropped to his belly, trying to be non-threatening. He rested his head on his front paws and looking up at her mournfully. Through their new mate bond he sent her a rapid flurry of emotions. Sadness. Grief. Loneliness. Love.

Suddenly the wolf shimmered and in an instant he saw Valerie's human form reappear, sitting naked on the forest floor. Her hair was matted with sweat, and the shadows under her eyes told Colt that she hadn't slept any better than he did last night.

Never sleep without your mate, his wolf lectured him.

She stared at him for a long time, her eyes unreadable. He could feel the sadness and nervousness coming off her in waves as she worked through her thoughts. Colt continued to lay still in his wolf form, watching her and waiting for her next move. Finally, she seemed to come to a decision.

"Your wolf looks as pathetic as mine feels," she finally said softly.

He slid forward on his belly and laid his head across her bare thighs. She sighed, and started stroking his head, right between his ears. It was the same spot he had rubbed him the first day he saw her, when he was brought to her clinic. It was his favorite spot, and he thumped his tail in pleasure.

Mate!

As they sat in silence he could feel something shift in her through the mate bond. Her anxiety eased, and she seemed to become almost calmer, more accepting.

"What am I going to do with you?" she whispered after several minutes of softly caressing his head.

Colt shifted in an instant, wolf turning into man. He looked up at her from his place on her lap with a hopeful smile.

"Love me?"

Valerie

It had been two weeks since Val had run into Colt in the woods. Somehow when their wolves met that night she finally accepted what her wolf had known right from the start: their being together was inevitable.

As she had sat in the woods stroking the silky fur between her mate's ears she finally decided to stop fighting her feelings. They had gone back to her place afterwards, and he spent the night. They had been together every night since then, alternating between their respective houses.

The more time they spent together, the stronger the mate bond between them became. It was like an invisible tether connecting them, bringing them completely in tune with each other, body and soul.

Val was trying very hard not to dwell on how serious they were getting so quickly. She might have accepted the inevitable but that didn't mean they had to rush into anything. Her human side was till urging caution, but it all felt natural when they were together. But then again, shifter relationships tended to move much faster than relationships between humans.

She had never thought she would want to live with a guy, but they were basically living together already. She found she didn't mind it. They got along well, and he was easy to live with, other than the way he never could seem to manage putting the lid back on the toothpaste tube.

As she had gotten to know Colt better, she realized that she really liked him as a person. They had enough in common that they could share some of their interests, but also were still different enough to keep it interesting. They had quickly become good friends.

And the sex, well that was off the charts. They were insatiable.

And yet, she held herself back, unable to give herself to him completely. She knew it. Colt knew it. She had not marked him back, despite her wolf's strong urging every time they made love. It wasn't one hundred percent necessary to bite him. Shifters often mated with humans who couldn't mark them back.

But it was symbolic for her to claim him and it still felt important to strengthen their bond and mark him for everyone to see. Just not quite yet.

Their feelings continued to grow stronger every day. Colt was much more affectionate than she was, always offering gentle touches while they were near each other, and telling her that he loved her at least once a day.

She knew he was hurt that she had not said the words to him yet. She couldn't say it back even though the fact was that she was totally, irreversibly in love with him.

Every time she was tempted to say the words, she could hear her mother justifying her father's bad behavior. "I love him," she said, every single time. "He's my mate."

Her phone rang and Val looked at the display. "Speak of the devil."

She swiped to answer. "Hi mom, how are you?"

"Fine sweetie," her mom answered, her voice sounding watery like she had been crying. As usual, Val ignored it. Whatever she was crying about no doubt involved her father. Nothing good could come of her hearing what her asshole father had done this time. She didn't need that kind of stress in her life.

Her mom chattered on for a while, catching her up on what was going on with her siblings, until she finally lost steam. "What's new with you Val?" she finally asked.

Colt walked in right at that moment, calling out "Hi honey, I'm home!" in a booming voice.

She rolled her eyes and motioned towards the phone at her ear.

"Who's that?" her mom asked curiously.

"Um, it's no one," she lied.

Colt sent her a hurt look and flopped on the couch next to her, clearly ready to eavesdrop. She stood up and paced across the room nervously.

"Are you dating someone?" her mom asked excitedly. "Did you finally find your mate?"

Val gripped the phone so tight she could hear the plastic case creaking in protest. She knew with Colt's shifter hearing he could hear mother as clearly as if he were on the call himself.

"I've got to go now, mom," she said.

"Valerie Ann Lupa, who is that man? You tell me what's going on right this instant!" Val's eyes widened in shock. Her mother was never forceful like that. She was usually meek as a mouse, thanks to her asshole father.

"Really? You're doing the mom voice on me?" Valerie asked in irritation. "I haven't even seen you in eighteen years. You don't get to mother me now."

"That was your decision, not mine," her mom snapped back. Val considered for the first time that her long absence had hurt her mother.

"You're the one who left here and never looked back," her mother reminded her in a wounded voice.

Colt's eyebrows raised. She had studiously avoided talking about her family and he had probably assumed they were dead or something.

"Are you going to tell her?" Colt asked loudly. Nosy, interfering mate.

"Tell me what?" her mom answered, confirming that she had heard Colt's words. Damn him for butting in like this. Why was he always pushing her? He knew that she liked to do things on her own timeline.

"Nothing mom. I just have a, um, new boyfriend and he's rudely interrupting."

She shot Colt a glare that would cow a lesser man. He just glared right back.

"Tell her."

"Tell me."

Val sighed, surrendering to the inevitable. "Fine. I um, well, um, the thing is, I did meet my mate." She met Colt's gaze. "His name is Colt."

Her mom squealed loudly, and Val winced, pulling her phone away from her ear.

"That's so wonderful honey. I can't wait to meet him!"

Colt stared at her, his expression indecipherable.

"Mom, can I call you tomorrow? I need to go."

"I bet you do," her mother said with a giggle. "I remember those early days of mating, when you can't keep your hands off each other."

"God mom, please!" Val protested. The last thing she needed was to think about her parents having sex. "I promise that I'll talk to you tomorrow."

She hung up and dropped her phone on the nearby shelf. She felt suddenly raw, like someone had flayed the skin off her. Meanwhile Colt stalked over towards her, his gaze as intense as she had ever seen it.

"Say it again," he ordered, his voice deep and demanding.

Val crossed her arms over her chest and gave him a saucy smile. "Say what?"

"Admit I'm your mate. Tell me you love me."

"Or what?" she asked.

He moved so fast he was a blur. In an instant Val found herself trapped against the wall, Colt's big body keeping her in place. He slapped her wrists up the wall over her head, holding them immobile with one big hand clamped around her wrists. She wiggled, but he had her trapped.

He leaned down and nipped her ear, then slid his mouth down to the scar from the mate bite. It was weirdly sensitive to touch, almost like another erogenous zone. She shivered as he laved it with his rough tongue, causing her clit to throb in time with his licking.

"Colt!"

He lifted his head and captured her lips. He kissed her deeply, dominating her with his tongue the same way he was dominating her body. By the time he pulled back they were both panting, vibrating with energy, the air thick with scent of their desire.

He met her eyes, and she could see his wolf lurking behind them. Her own wolf pranced happily.

Mate! Bite him. Tell him how we feel!

They were silent for a full minute before Val finally gave him the words he had been waiting for almost since they met.

"I do love you Colt," she admitted. "But my worst nightmare is turning into my mother, and I swear to god, if you ever hurt me I will castrate you. Just remember, I'm a vet, and I know multiple ways to do it."

"You're so hot when you're violent," he said, his gaze intense.

She looked up towards the ceiling. "Why couldn't I get a less annoying mate?"

He kissed her forehead tenderly.

"I don't know what happened when you were a kid Valerie, and I hope you'll tell me some time," he said tenderly. "But I promise you this: I. Will. Never. Hurt. You. There will be no need for castration. I love you and I will happily spend every day for the rest of my life proving that to you."

She could see the truth in his eyes and finally, she did what her wolf had been begging her to do since the moment they had first laid eyes on him in the vet clinic. She lowered her head and pressed her lips against his neck, slowly releasing her fangs. She bit through the skin, down to the muscle, marking him as hers forever.

As she finally gave Colt the claiming bite, she felt connected to him in way she never had before.

"Mate!" she said, licking his wound closed. "You're stuck with me now. How about we consummate this thing?"

Epilogue - Colt

Five months later...

"Are you wolves ready for the most incredible game night ever?"

Susan threw open the door with a wide smile. "I promise you it will be epic."

Val laughed and drew her friend in for a quick hug. "We brought pot stickers."

Colt followed behind her, trading a secret smile with Susan.

Val moved towards the dining room table where they usually played their board games but stopped suddenly as she caught sight of the table. Instead of board games the table was covered with a linen tablecloth and candles. Two sets of place settings were arranged in one corner, wine glasses on either side.

"What's this?" she asked in confusion.

"Surprise!" Colt said jubilantly.

"Surprise what?"

"It's our six month anniversary," Colt told her.

"Huh?"

Behind him Susan laughed, muttering beneath her breath. "Doesn't have a romantic bone in her body, this woman."

She scuttled out to the kitchen. Susan was a professional chef and Colt had enlisted her in planning a surprise celebration for their six month anniversary.

Valerie had moved into his place four months ago and rented out the apartment over the clinic to one of her vet techs. Instead of taking her to a restaurant he and Susan thought it would be more fun to surprise Valerie with a private anniversary dinner at Susan's house.

Susan had cooked a feast to help them celebrate, then she was going to go stay at her boyfriend's house, leaving them to have the space to themselves.

"OK, so dinner is all set up in warming trays in the kitchen," Susan told them. "Just pile the dishes in the sink when you're done, I'll get them in the morning."

She gave them each a hug. "Enjoy your anniversary dinner. Just don't have sex on my counters please."

Val turned to him as Susan scuttled out. Her brow was crinkled in confusion. He gently pushed her into a chair and poured them each a glass of wine.

"What anniversary is this exactly?" she asked.

"Six months ago, today I fell off a cliff, was hit by a car, and then was struck by the thunderbolt of love."

"Oh my god," she rolled her eyes. "Did you really just say that?"

They had long ago realized that Colt was the romantic one in their relationship. It was OK, he loved his pragmatic mate just as she was.

Colt slid off his chair and dropped to one knee. He took her hand in his and stroked her wrist with his thumb.

"What are you doing?" she asked, watching him warily.

Suddenly he felt nervous. He hoped she wasn't about to freak out. He reached into the pocket of his jacket and pulled out a blue box, opening it up to show her the ring inside.

He knew Val wouldn't want a fussy ring, so he had chosen a plain silver band inlaid with tiny diamonds. Something that wouldn't get caught on her surgical gloves or in the fur of some animal patient she was treating.

"Valerie, I love having you as my mate, but would you do me the honor of also becoming my wife?"

"We're doing this now?" she clarified. "Mating and marriage, making it official?"

He nodded. "Yes we are."

"Hmm. OK then."

He cocked his head. "OK? You really know how to wound a guy. Can I get a little enthusiasm here? I mean, I planned this whole thing."

Valerie laughed and dropped to her knees in front of him, reaching for the ring. "I'm sorry sweetie, you just caught me by surprise."

She slid the engagement ring onto the third finger and studied it with a smile. "I love this ring Colt. And I love you. So yes, what the hell, let's make our mating even more official and get hitched."

Inside his mind, his wolf thumped his tail happily. *First wedding, then pups.*

All in due time, he told his wolf. *All in due time.*

Did you like this story? Show the love and leave me a review. Reviews are like puppies, they make you feel happy.

Be sure to keep reading for a special except from "Until You Came Along", available now on select online bookstores.

Special Preview

Until You Came Along by Rose Bak

Jen heard the rumbling from all the way in the kitchen. Wiping her hands on a towel, she walked to the front porch to watch the two large buses drive up the long driveway to the farmhouse. Belching smoke, they idled and came to a stop, one behind the other.

Although it wasn't even 10 a.m. yet the sun shone brightly in the summer sky, showcasing the dust left in the wake of the parked buses. A bird squawked loudly in the sudden silence as a serious looking young woman scurried out of the first bus, glasses askew, a clipboard gripped in one hand, cellphone in another. Two large mountains of men followed her, hulking shadows.

"Jen Oliver? The band is here. We'll just come in and...." she moved to enter the house, but Jen stood her ground, blocking the door.

"Where are they?" she asked the woman, her tone icy. "And who are you exactly?"

The woman looked flustered for a brief moment before her stern mask fell back down again. She shuffled her cell phone into the hand with the clipboard and stuck out her now-free hand to shake. "I'm Simone. I manage the band."

Jen ignored her hand. "Well, manage them out of those buses. They don't get to send the help out to greet their sister."

Simone looked confused as she dropped her hand back to her side. "They're all sleeping. They had a late night. We'll just come in and check...."

"Still up all night and sleeping all day, huh? That's been the same since they were teenagers." Jen shook her head. On the farm they had all been taught the value of hard work – up before dawn, work all day, and early to bed. Somehow those lessons hadn't really stuck with her brothers despite her grandparents' best efforts over the years.

Of course, the boys, as she still thought of them, had been away from the farm for ten years now, chasing fame and fortune as the biggest boy band to hit the charts since N Sync. Like the band that came before them, the Oliver Boys had grown up but continued to enchant teenage girls across the world with their pop tunes.

Simone clearly felt protective of the boys. "They played last night in Wichita you know," she said sternly. "The show went until almost midnight, then they met the fans and press for hours after."

"By meet the fans and press do you mean got drunk and partied?" Jen's tone did little to hide her opinion of the boys and their reputation for debauched partying.

Simone shook her head. "They've mostly settled down now. There's not as much partying as there used to be when they were younger. But they still need to make an effort to meet people, it's part of the job. Now we'll just come in and...."

Jen shook her head. "Well," she drawled. "When they wake up from their so-called job, you send them on in. The rest of you need to find some other place to bunk. I'm not running a hotel for drunken roadies here."

A slight movement behind Simone caught Jen's eyes. One of the giant men flanking Simone shook with repressed laughter, his mouth twisted in a smirk but his face otherwise impassive. Jen looked at him for the first time. He was the size of a small tank, several inches over 6 feet tall, with impossibly wide shoulders and large biceps. His hair was a dark blond, "dishwater blonde" her grandma would call it, worn military short. He was dressed all in black, and she noticed a gun on the shoulder holster. Jen wondered why he felt he needed a gun out here in the middle of nowhere. She felt him watching her and she raised her eyes to his, a shiver of awareness coursing through her, although she couldn't make out his eyes behind the dark sunglasses.

"Miss Oliver..." Simone started again.

"Jen"

"OK, then, Jen, we need to do a security sweep before the boys come in. If you could just move aside, we'll get started." Simone nodded decisively.

"A security—-what the hell are you talking about?"

Simone turned to the man who'd been staring at Jen earlier. "This is Nick, he's head of security for the band. He'll be doing a security sweep and assessment with Brian here," she pointed at the second silent man.

"We don't need a security sweep. This place is as safe as it comes. We don't even lock the doors in these parts."

Simone shook her head again, vibrating with irritation and clearly not used to people disobeying her orders. "No way. The boys don't go anywhere without a security check ahead of time. I'm afraid I have to insist."

Jen shot her a look filled with venom, her tone as cold as ice. "You can insist all you like but this is my property. You have no right to it, and neither do the boys. Y'all can just run along now, I'm not having some ginormous strangers poking around my property. Don't make me sic the dogs on you." Simone's mouth dropped open.

This was an empty threat. Jen's three dogs looked mean, but they were incurably friendly. They were just as likely to lick a person to death as bite them. Jen had a sneaking suspicion that if someone tried to kill her the dogs would jump over her body and leave with the killer. But these music people didn't need to know that. If there was one thing Jen hated, it was music people. They were way too self-important and proud.

"Excuse me ma'am," the guy called Nick interrupted.

"Jen," she repeated, a trace of irritation in her tone.

He inclined his head. "Sorry. Jen. As Simone mentioned, I'm head of security for the band. We've had some issues and I would be very appreciative if my team could just poke around for a bit and make sure there's nothing amiss." His tone was deferential and charming, which only heightened Jen's suspicions.

"What kind of issues?"

"I'm afraid I'm not at liberty to discuss that ma—I mean Jen."

"Then I'm afraid I'm not at liberty to grant you access to my property. You step foot off that driveway, and I'll shoot you myself, right after I set the dogs on you. And you," she pointed at Simone, "better make sure no one bothers me again until I see those boys on my porch." She spun on her heel and slammed the door. It was going to be a long day.

For more of Jen's story, check out Until You Came Along by Rose Bak. Available at select online retailers.

About the Author

Rose Bak has been obsessed with reading since she got her first library card at age five. A passionate reader and a frequent blogger, she writes both fiction and nonfiction. Rose lives in the Pacific Northwest with her family and special needs dogs.

Please sign up for my newsletter[1] to get a free book and keep up to date on all the Rose Bak romance news.

---

1. *https://storyoriginapp.com/giveaways/62ee758e-068f-11eb-904e-c373f6014fe1*

Other Books by Rose Bak

The Diamond Bay Contemporary Romance Series
    Brand New Penny
    Fresh as a Daisy
    Right as Rain
    The Good with Numbers Holiday Novella Contemporary Romance Series:
    Love Unmasked
    The Thanksgiving Scrooge
    Maid for Christmas
    Countdown to Love
    Valentine's Lottery
    The Oliver Boys Band Contemporary Romance Series:
    Until You Came Along
    Rock Star Teacher
    Rock Star Writer
    Rock Star Neighbor
    Beach Wedding

Non-fiction
    What to Do If You Find a Cougar in Your Living Room: Self-Care in an Uncaring World

Catch up with these and other stories. Join my newsletter for more information[1] or follow my author page on your favorite retailer.

---

1. https://storyoriginapp.com/giveaways/62ee758e-068f-11eb-904e-c373f6014fe1